Chinenye is a new children's storybook author. Ms Purplebubble's Class (a children's book series) Book 1, is her first published children's storybook.

MS PURPLEBUBBLE'S CLASS – BOOK 1

THE NEW PUPIL

CHINENYE SANTINA EBUKA-UGWU

AUSTIN MACAULEY PUBLISHERS™
LONDON • CAMBRIDGE • NEW YORK • SHARJAH

A CIP catalogue record for this title is available from the British Library.

ISBN 9781398457683 (Paperback)
ISBN 9781398457690 (Hardback)
ISBN 9781398459342 (ePub e-book)
ISBN 9781398459335 (Audiobook)

www.austinmacauley.com

First Published 2022
Austin Macauley Publishers Ltd®
1 Canada Square
Canary Wharf
London
E14 5AA

To all the Children in the world, You are special and beautiful. May you always be kind and show love to one another.

Special thanks to my husband and children for all their love and encouragement, you are my world and I love you unconditionally. To my parents, who first taught me love, kindness and compassion through their exemplary life, I feel so blessed being your daughter and I love you dearly.

It was Friday morning and Tinkin had just woken up.

He tidied his bed, then went to see his parents.

"Good morning Mum and Dad," he said.

"Good morning son," they replied.

With a big smile on his face,
Tinkin went off to prepare for school.

He was really excited at breakfast because it was nearly the weekend, and he would get to play with his friends in the park.

After breakfast, Tinkin said goodbye to his parents and went off to school.

The school bus arrived as he walked outside, so Tinkin hopped on. He loved the school bus because he got to see all his friends.

SCHOOL BUS
SCHOOL BUS

"Hello Tinkin," his friends cheered.

"Hello! It is nice to see you all today," replied Tinkin with a smile on his face.

Tinkin was the most popular kid in school. Everyone liked him because he was so kind and always willing to help others.

When they got to school,

SCHOOL
School Bus

Ms Purplebubble, their class teacher, was waiting for them in their classroom. She told them that there was a new pupil joining them named Divine.

Divine had long brown curly hair and she was so pretty, like a princess. She was a bit different from the other children in her class because she could not walk, so she used a wheelchair.

Ms Purplebubble introduced Divine to the other children in class.

"Good morning children, this is Divine," said Ms Purplebubble.

Divine looked away and her face went red. She was a bit shy.

All the children said hello with a friendly smile.

Divine smiled looking down at her shoes and her face turned red again.

Tinkin then walked towards her and introduced himself.

"Hi, I am Tinkin. Should I show you to your desk?" he asked.

"Sure, I would love that." Divine smiled and thanked him.

Tinkin showed Divine her desk just next to his.

When it was playtime, all the children went out to the play garden to play.

Ms Purplebubble brought apple pie for the children. She cut the apple pie into slices and took it to the play garden. Each of the children had a slice.

There was also a slice of apple pie left for Divine. She came a little bit late to the play garden because she had to put all her things away in her school bag.

When Divine got to the play garden, she was about to take her slice of apple pie. But she accidently knocked over the plate!

Down went the pie. "Oh no! I don't have any pie to eat now," she cried.

The children munched on their apple pie slices,

Divine sat alone at a corner in the play garden watching them.

Tinkin saw Divine and went over to her.

"Hi Divine, would you like some apple pie?
We could share mine," he said with a smile.

"That's very kind. Thank you, Tinkin,"
she replied with an even bigger smile.

They both enjoyed sharing the delicious apple pie.

All the other children looked at Tinkin and thought he was so generous. They realised they also needed to be kinder to Divine.

When play time was over, all the children went back to class.

Tinkin went back to class with Divine showing her around as they went.

Ms Purplebubble was so pleased with Tinkin. He was setting a good example by being friendly to Divine.

Ms Purplebubble told the class that you always need to be kind, so that others will be kind back.

Tinkin was excited when he got a gold star sticker for good behaviour from Ms Purplebubble.

2×1=2
2×2=4
2×3=?
WELL
DONE
TINKIN

When school was over, Tinkin's mum came to pick him up and she met Divine.

"Mum, this is Divine. It was her first day today at our school and I have been showing her around," said Tinkin.

"Hello Divine, it is so nice to meet you. I hope you enjoyed your first day," said Tinkin's mum.

"I sure did, thank you. Tinkin helped me a lot. It was an easy first day for me," replied Divine.

Tinkin's mum smiled and they all said their goodbyes.

SCHOOL BUS
SCHOOL BUS

At home, Tinkin showed his mum the shiny gold star sticker he had been given.

WELL
DONE
TINKIN

“That’s so wonderful,” said Tinkin’s mum. “I’m so proud of you. It’s important to be kind to people even if they are different.”

“Thanks mum,” replied Tinkin. “Can I go play?”

“Of course, you can,” said his mum with a warm smile.

WELL
DONE
TINKIN

Tinkin skipped off happily. He couldn't wait to play with all his friends in the park.

THE END